MAKE FOUR MILLION DOLLAR$ BY NEXT THUR$DAY!

MAKE FOUR MILLION DOLLAR$ BY NEXT THUR$DAY!

By STEPHEN MANES

Illustrated by George Ulrich

A BANTAM SKYLARK BOOK
NEW YORK • TORONTO • LONDON • SYDNEY • AUCKLAND

MAKE FOUR MILLION DOLLARS BY NEXT THURSDAY!

A Bantam Skylark Book / February 1991

*Skylark Books is a registered trademark of Bantam Books, a division of
Bantam Doubleday Dell Publishing Group, Inc. Registered in U.S. Patent
and Trademark Office and elsewhere.*

Library of Congress Cataloging-in-Publication Data

Manes, Stephen
    Make four million dollars by next Thursday! / by Stephen Manes.
        p.   cm.
    Summary: Jason attracts a lot of attention when he starts following the zany
advice in a get-rich-quick book by the bizarre Dr. Silverfish.
    ISBN 0-553-07050-9
    [1. Money—Fiction. 2. Humorous stories.]   I. Title.
PZ7.M31264Mak   1990
[Fic]—dc20   90-34711
                                                                              CIP
                                                                               AC

Published simultaneously in the United States and Canada

---

*Bantam Books are published by Bantam Books, a division of Bantam Doubleday Dell
Publishing Group, Inc. Its trademark, consisting of the words "Bantam Books" and the
portrayal of a rooster, is Registered in U.S. Patent and Trademark Office and in other
countries. Marca Registrada. Bantam Books, 666 Fifth Avenue, New York, New York
10103.*

PRINTED IN THE UNITED STATES OF AMERICA

BVG   0   9   8   7   6   5   4   3   2

For Susan

MAKE FOUR MILLION DOLLAR$ BY NEXT THUR$DAY!

1

Some people want to be doctors or lawyers
or pig farmers. Jason Nozzle wanted to be a
multimillionaire.

It all began one Thursday afternoon at the
Frozen Lizard stand in the park. Jason had just
ordered an Iced Iguana bar. But when he
reached into his pocket, his money was missing.
In its place was a hole the size of his fist. His
allowance for the entire month had disappeared—
every last cent.

Jason was pretty sure he had the money when
school let out. But ever since, he and his best
friend Ravi had been roaming through the park
woods. The money could have fallen out anywhere. "Twelve whole dollars!" Jason said de-
jectedly. "Gone!"

"I'll help you look for it," Ravi offered, biting the head off a Cool Chameleon.

Jason sighed. "It'd take forever. We wouldn't even know where to start looking."

"You're right," Ravi agreed. "And who knows? Maybe somebody else already found your money —and kept it. Maybe you should just forget it."

But Jason couldn't just forget that much money. There had to be some way to get it back. As he trudged along, he tried to think of what might work. Suddenly he had a brainstorm.

Jason ran home to borrow his brother's treasure finder. When it found metal, it was supposed to beep. Jason hoped it would beep at his quarters, dimes, and nickels. He hoped the trail of coins would lead him to his two five-dollar bills and two singles.

The treasure finder began beeping the minute Jason walked into the woods. *Beep!* A rusty old tailpipe covered with moss. *Boop!* Three smelly sardine cans with bugs crawling out of them. *Braap!* A ballpoint pen sticking out of some mud.

Jason bent down to pick it up. It wasn't even a whole pen.

"Pointless!" he exclaimed, tossing it at the sardine cans. "Some treasure!"

Beep! Boop! Broooop! The loudest treasure yet! "Probably another hunk of junk," Jason muttered. He stooped down to take a look.

Junk, all right: a battered metal table—bent, twisted, upside down, and missing two legs. Treasure? Ha! Forget it!

But Jason spotted a green dollar sign sticking out beneath the tabletop. Was it some of his missing money? He pushed the table aside and bent down closer.

Jason shook his head in disgust. "Just my rotten luck!" The dollar sign wasn't printed on money at all. It was printed on the front of a book.

Jason picked up the book and wiped the mud from the front cover. There were dollar signs all over it. There were even dollar signs in the title: *Make Four Million Dollar$ by Next Thur$day!*

The author's picture was on the back. Dr. K. Pinkerton Silverfish was wearing a worn-out baseball cap with a dollar sign on the front, two untied shoes with dollar bills for tongues, and a grimy apron that said "I Eat Rich Food." His shirt was decorated with brightly colored dollar signs. In front of it a big golden dollar-sign pendant dangled from a chain of pennies. Dr. Silverfish was wearing glasses with dollar-sign frames. He was biting into a bologna sandwich shaped like a dollar sign, and he was barbecuing an enormous jack-o'-lantern that had dollar signs for eyes.

Jason snorted. He had seen plenty of rich people on TV and in newspapers and magazines. Rich people didn't look anything like Dr. Silverfish. Rich people had expensive cars. Rich people had enormous mansions. Rich people wore clothes that fit them perfectly and had designer names on the front or the back— sometimes the front *and* the back. If you had to pick someone to teach you how to become a millionaire, Dr. Silverfish would probably come in last.

But Jason opened the book anyway. It couldn't do any worse than the treasure finder. And maybe, just maybe, Dr. Silverfish was smarter and richer than he looked.

CHAPTER ONE

A Word from the Expert!

I, Dr. K. Pinkerton Silverfish, happen to be the world's greatest expert on getting rich quick. But you know what steams my clams? You know what frosts my mug?
You think I look silly! That's what!

Jason grinned. Dr. Silverfish was smart enough to get *that* right.

Well, maybe I do. So what? I wear a comfortable old baseball cap and leave my shoes untied and barbecue jack-o'-lanterns because I want to—and tough pumpkins to anybody who doesn't like it!
When you have four million dollars, you can, too! Or you can do something else—though I can't imagine why.

Jason thought he probably would do something else. But he kept on reading.

CHAPTER TWO

Why Only Four Million Dollars?
Why Not Four Billion?

Many of you have no doubt read my wonderful, brilliant, and best-selling book, *Be a Perfect Person in Just Three Days!* In it I, Dr. K. Pinkerton Silverfish, personally recommended my new book, *Make Four Billion Dollars by Next Thursday!* Well, this book *is* that new book—with one slight change!

So you may be wondering why this book just teaches you how to make a measly four million dollars instead of four billion. You may feel disappointed. You may feel shortchanged. You may feel gypped. If so, *too bad for you!*

As the world's leading authority on multimillionairedom, I believe that four million dollars is more than plenty for any individual on this planet— except for one or two incredibly greedy people I will not stoop to mention. So if you think you just can't possibly get along with a mere four million dollars, *PUT THIS BOOK DOWN*

*IMMEDIATELY, YOU INCREDIBLY
GREEDY PERSON, YOU!*

Jason thought for a second. He decided four
million dollars would be enough for him.

CHAPTER THREE

The Silverfish Road to Riches

**Still here? Good. I am now going to
start you on your personal four-million-
dollar plan. All you have to do is follow
my instructions *precisely* from now until
next Thursday. When you wake up
that morning, you will be rich, and I
will be proud to welcome you to the
ranks of four-millionaires.**

Jason turned the page.

Bam! A giant boxing glove popped out of the
book and socked Jason in the nose. It was only
paper, a pop-up trick, so it didn't hurt at all.
But it wasn't exactly something Jason had
expected.

The boxing glove had a message printed on
it:

DID I TELL YOU
TO TURN THE PAGE?

Jason shook his head.

Correct. I most certainly did not.
But I'll let it go just this once. Re-
member, you must follow my instruc-
tions *precisely*. So don't go turning any
more pages until I tell you to. Got
it?

Jason nodded.

Good. Please fold this boxing glove
neatly and turn the page.

Jason followed the instructions very, very
carefully.

Fine. Read the next two senten-
ces and close the book. Sentence
One: This evening after dinner,
please return to the very next
page. Sentence Two: See you later,
future four-millionaire!

Jason shut the book. Future four-millionaire? He could hardly believe it. He could hardly even imagine it.

With four million dollars, he would never have to worry about losing his allowance through holes in his pockets. He would never have to worry about money at all. He could buy anything he wanted—probably *everything* he wanted.

He could buy slick new clothes and wild new shoes and a portable CD player and a season ticket for every sport and two or three enormous-screen TV sets. He could buy cassettes of movies instead of renting them at the video store. He could buy a computer and all the game cartridges in the world.

He could buy every baseball card ever printed. He could buy enough baseballs so that when one rolled down the sewer, he wouldn't have to get all messy trying to get it back. Maybe he could even buy his own ballpark. And he'd probably still have money to spare.

The more he thought about it, the better it sounded. He could buy a fast car and hire somebody to drive him around. He could buy an airplane and learn how to fly like a kid he

saw on TV. He could buy a yacht and sail around the world.

Instead of Jason asking his mom for money, his mom would ask *him*. Maybe he'd even give her an allowance. But if his big brother Stewart asked for money, Jason would make him beg a little. In a lot of ways, that sounded like the best part of all.

Being a four-millionaire was definitely something to look forward to, all right. Jason tucked the book under his arm and headed home.

Then he stopped and turned off the treasure finder. It had done its job, even if only by accident. There was no point wasting batteries trying to hunt for lost nickels and dimes and quarters and five-dollar bills when four million dollars were just one week away.

2

"Find anything?" his brother Stewart called from the kitchen as Jason came through the front door.

Jason had no intention of mentioning Dr. Silverfish's book. "Yeah!" he shouted back. "A lot of junk!"

He hid the book in the living room under the middle sofa cushion. If Stewart saw it, he'd probably grab it for himself. Jason was not about to let that happen until he became a four-millionaire—and probably not even then.

Jason walked into the kitchen. "Remember," Stewart told him, "when you use that thing, you owe me for batteries. They're expensive."

Jason shrugged. "I know." He smiled to himself. Expensive batteries wouldn't be a problem after next Thursday. Expensive *anything* wouldn't be a problem.

Jason raided the cupboard. He took out a tomato-zucchini honey-granola yogurt bar and a couple of cauliflower chocolate chip cookies. He poured himself a glass of cranberry-rutabaga-broccoli juice.

He stopped by the sofa to pick up Dr. Silverfish's book and went to his room to start on his homework. But for some reason it was harder than usual.

Jason tried to practice spelling, but every word seemed to be spelled *m-i-l-l-i-o-n-a-i-r-e*. He tried to work on geography, but he kept seeing dollar signs where state capitals should be. He tried to do his math, but no matter what the problem was, the answer always came out *$4,000,000.00*.

Not even dinner kept him from thinking about four million dollars. "What kind of stuff do millionaires eat?" he blurted out to his mom and brother.

"Not much need for you to worry about that." Stewart laughed.

"Why not?" Jason demanded. "Maybe I'll be a millionaire someday."

"Yeah," Stewart chortled. "The day after I fly to Mars in my pajamas."

Jason decided to ignore him. "What *do* millionaires eat?" he asked his mom.

"Caviar," his brother broke in. "Fish eggs."

Jason made a face.

"Seriously," Stewart said. "I saw it on that TV show, *Rich People and Their Expensive Stuff.* The fish eggs look like little ball bearings, only squishy. They cost five hundred dollars a pound. Millionaires are supposed to love 'em."

"Yuck!" Jason exclaimed. "I wonder if they *taste* like squishy ball bearings."

"I guess you'll just have to wait till you're a millionaire to find out," Stewart teased. "And that'll be one long wait."

"Maybe not," Jason said with his mouth full.

"Yeah, right," Stewart scoffed. "Next thing, you'll tell us you'll make ten zillion dollars by next weekend or something. What an imagination!"

"Enough, you two," said Mrs. Nozzle. "We're a long, long way from being millionaires, and I certainly don't expect that to change anytime soon. Now, finish your tofu and peapod casserole, or no cream cheese and bean sprout pudding."

But Jason was already wolfing down his tofu. He was in a hurry to finish dinner. He had an important four-million-dollar matter to take care of.

When Jason walked into his room, Dr. K. Pinkerton Silverfish stared at him from the back of the book. Suddenly Jason had a burning desire to find out more about this Silverfish guy. For one thing, he wondered what the *K.* stood for. He opened the book carefully and read the back jacket flap:

ABOUT THE AUTHOR

Dr. K. Pinkerton Silverfish is the world's greatest authority on getting rich quick. This has been confirmed again and again by such experts as Professor K. P. S. Ilverfish, world-famous authority on multimillionairedom.

Dr. Silverfish holds the Loot and Plunder Chair at the School of Fort Knox, except when he puts it on the floor and sits down on it. He owns the world's fourth-largest private collection of slow-roasted jack-o'-lanterns.

Dr. Silverfish has donated hundreds

of three-dollar bills to dozens of worthy causes. Although he refuses to divulge what the *K*. stands for, he claims it is definitely *not* Kumpelstiltskin.

So much for the *K*., Jason thought. But as long as the book was right in his hands there was no sense delaying even a moment longer. Jason opened it to where he'd left off.

CHAPTER FOUR

Your Personal Four-Million-Dollar Plan

Hi! Yo! Howdy! Welcome back! Good to see you!

You are about to begin the first step of your march to multimillionairedom. But first you will need the Three P's of Prosperity: Pen—one bold marker; Paper—37 sheets; and Pins—37 safety.

Jason stared at the page. He couldn't imagine what Dr. Silverfish had in mind.

**Well, what are you waiting for? Do
you want to make four million dollars
or don't you? Go get the pen, paper,
and pins *right now!***

Jason had no trouble finding the pen or the
paper right at his desk. But only his mom would
know where the safety pins were.

As usual most evenings, Mrs. Nozzle was
hard at work at the dining room table beside a
huge stack of papers. "Do we have any safety
pins?" Jason asked as she punched some but-
tons on her calculator.

"In my sewing basket, I think," Mrs. Nozzle
said without looking up.

"I need them *now*," Jason pleaded. "It's for
homework."

The calculator beeped rudely. Mrs. Nozzle
glared at Jason. "Check the top of my dresser.
If the sewing basket's not there, holler."

As Jason scurried out of the room, his mom
called after him. "What kind of homework is
this, anyway? Are you going to learn to sew?"

"Right," Jason mumbled to himself. "I'm sewing up four million dollars. Pinning it down."
But he didn't let his mother hear a word.

The sewing basket was on the dresser—right beside some baby pictures of Jason and his brother. Jason stuck out his tongue at the pictures. He hated his mother thinking of him as some sort of baby. He bet she wouldn't think of him that way once he became a four-millionaire!

Jason found the safety pins and took them back to his room. He closed the door and picked up the book.

Got everything you need?

Jason nodded.

Excellent. Now on both sides of every sheet of paper, draw the biggest, boldest dollar signs that will fit. When you're done, turn the page.

Jason had no idea how drawing dollar signs on pieces of paper could possibly make him rich. But since following instructions was absolutely essential, Jason picked up the marker. He drew big dollar signs thirty-seven times on the front sides and thirty-seven times on the backs. He picked up the book and turned the page.

> **Lucky you! You now have seventy-four dollars. See how easy it is to make money?**

Jason scowled.

> **Ho, ho, ho! Ha, ha, ha! Whoooeee! Sorry. That was a little getting-rich-quick joke. Please excuse me. What you have, of course, is not seventy-four dollars, but seventy-four dollar *signs*. There's a big difference.**

"I'll say," Jason muttered.

> **Your dollar signs won't buy you anything, but they will soon come in very handy indeed. So put them in a safe place where nothing can disturb them —along with all thirty-seven safety pins.**

Jason hid the dollar signs in the middle drawer of his desk. He counted out thirty-seven pins and put them in the drawer too. He went back to the book.

Whew! That was exhausting! I need a rest.

And so do you. It'll be good practice. Multimillionaires take time off whenever they get the chance.

Fortunately, the Silverfish Four-Million-Dollar Method is so foolproof there's no need to rush into it. The rest of the course begins bright and early next Monday. Rise and shine half an hour earlier than usual that morning. Then (and *only* then—no peeking!) read the very next page of this book before you do anything else at all.

From now until Monday you may do whatever you choose—though I personally recommend thinking about all the pumpkins four million dollars will buy you. See you next week!

Next week! Jason didn't think he could possibly wait that long to find out what he'd have to do next to become a four-millionaire. But he couldn't risk peeking ahead, because he was sure Dr. Silverfish would find out—and maybe even play a dirty trick on him. He closed the book and put it in the drawer with the dollar signs and the pins.

Suddenly Jason's head was filled with zeroes—the ones that came right after a dollar sign and a four:

$4,000,000

Then he saw even more zeroes, the ones for cents. Four million dollars seemed even bigger when you counted every penny:

$4,000,000.00

For the next three days, Jason daydreamed and nightdreamed about dollar signs. He dreamed about zeroes. He dreamed about all the stuff he could buy. He dreamed about expensive fish eggs that tasted like squishy ball bearings. He did not dream about pumpkins—not even once.

3

Cock-a-doodle-*grrrrowf!* Jason's Monster Rooster alarm clock crowed and growled him awake bright and early Monday morning. He rubbed his eyes. He went to his desk. He took out Dr. Silverfish's book and opened it up.

Good morning! Welcome back! Get those dollar signs and safety pins ready!

Jason took them from the drawer and put them on top of his desk.

Now use the safety pins to fasten every last dollar sign to the clothes you're going to wear today. Be sure

to use the pins. Do not even *think* of using bubble gum!

It is absolutely essential that you use every single dollar sign. You must have at least ten of them on each article of clothing you wear, except for your underwear, your shoes, and your socks. No excuses will be accepted. You must wear them from breakfast until after dinner.

See you then—same time, same book, future four-millionaire!

Jason followed the instructions. On his clothes the dollar signs looked almost like feathers. When he was finished, the dollar-sign-feathered outfit looked downright ridiculous. He left it on his bed and went into the bathroom.

He tried not to think about it as he brushed his teeth. "Don't take all week in there!" his brother shouted through the door.

"Malmoshdun!" Jason hollered back through a mouthful of toothpaste. He decided that the first thing he would do with his four million dollars was build his own personal private bathroom.

"Turtle! Slug! Snail!" Stewart snapped when Jason came out the door. But Jason didn't answer back. He just strutted proudly into his room. By Thursday he'd be a four-millionaire. Poor Stewart would find out who the slug was *then*.

But Jason stopped strutting when he saw his dollar-sign outfit. He put on his underwear and his socks. He fidgeted around.

"Hurry up!" his mother shouted. Jason sighed. It was too late to stall anymore.

He pulled his shirt on carefully, so he wouldn't tear any of the dollar signs. Then he put on his dollar-feathered pants.

He looked at himself in the mirror. The outfit made Jason look like some sort of giant dollar-bird. If he had been looking at anyone else, he would have laughed out loud. Instead he took a deep breath and headed for the kitchen.

Stewart was eating cereal and reading the paper. Mrs. Nozzle was watching a TV exercise program without doing the exercises. Maybe, Jason hoped, just maybe, they'd be so busy they wouldn't look his way.

He tried to move quietly, but his dollar-feathers rustled a bit as he slipped into his chair.

They rustled even more as he reached across the table and grabbed the cereal box.

Jason poured the Tooth Busters as quietly as possible. But when he added the milk, they made their famous jawbreaking lightning cracks and earthquake rumbles. His mother heard the commotion and looked up from the TV.

"Jason!" she shrieked. "What in the world are you wearing?"

"A pair of pants and a T-shirt," Jason replied truthfully. "Some underwear. Socks. The usual."

"But what is that all over you?" she demanded.

Stewart peeked over the sports section. "Oh, no! It's a bird!" He laughed. "It's a dodo!" He laughed harder. "It's Super Loon!" And he laughed so hard his chair nearly toppled over backwards.

Jason tried to ignore him. "We're . . . uh . . . doing something special in history class," he stammered.

"I know! You're a passenger pigeon!" his brother guessed. "They became extinct because people shot them for money."

"No, I'm not," Jason replied, stalling for time. "I'm . . . uh . . . the national debt."

Stewart turned two of his fingers into scissors and aimed them at Jason's dollar-feathers. "What are you doing?" Jason cried, jumping away.

"I'm cutting the national debt!" Stewart proclaimed.

"Stop that!" Jason shouted.

"Yes, stop it, Stewart," Mrs. Nozzle agreed. "Don't mess up your brother's costume." She turned to Jason. "How much *is* the national debt?"

"I—um—don't remember," Jason stammered. "A lot."

"Trillions of dollars," his brother declared. "If you really did this right, you'd have so many dollars on you, you'd suffocate to death."

Very funny, Jason thought. We'll see how many jokes you make about me when I'm a four-millionaire!

Jason finished his breakfast and carefully hoisted his bookbag to his back. He took a deep breath and strolled out to the sidewalk.

Just up the street, his friend Ravi came out his front door. "What's going on?" he said with a smirk. "I thought Halloween was in October."

Jason scowled. "Some people wear designer

labels on their clothes. I'm wearing dollar signs, okay?"

"No," said Ravi. "It's not okay. It's weird. I don't get it."

"You don't have to get it," Jason told him. "It's a top secret mission. I can't tell you about it. So don't even ask, okay?"

Ravi shrugged. "Okay. Super. Fine with me," he said so that Jason knew he didn't mean it. But at least Ravi behaved like a friend and changed the subject instead of making a big deal about Jason's outfit.

Which was more than Jason could say for most people. All day long, kids came up to him and tried to pull off his dollar signs. They asked him if he had change for a twenty. They called him names like "dollar-featherhead" and "money-birdbrain."

Even his teachers got into the act. His math teacher said Jason might have a whole lot of dollars, but he didn't seem to have any sense. His history teacher made him turn around and then acted disappointed because Jason didn't have a green back. His science teacher suggested that Jason should change his name to

William so that people could call him Dollar Bill. The class howled again and again.

But when the teachers asked Jason to take off the dollar signs, he insisted he had to wear them. He had made a deal with a pen pal in a foreign country, Jason said, and he couldn't exactly explain why, because it was supposed to be a secret, but his pen pal halfway around the world was doing the very same thing, only with his own kind of foreign money rather than dollars. It was a project for international goodwill, sort of.

The teachers didn't seem to believe him. They told him to sit down and try to keep from rustling.

But the worst part was gym. Remembering Dr. Silverfish's orders, Jason took the dollar signs off his shirt and pants and pinned them to his gym outfit. It made him late for class.

The coach was not impressed. "One push-up for every dollar!" he boomed. And when Jason had trouble climbing the ropes, one of the kids said, "Just flap your wings and fly!"

Jason was very glad when the bell rang at the end of last period. All the way home, kids from other classes kept pointing at him and laughing. Not the kids from his own class; they were all laughed out. For once Jason was actually delighted to get to his room and work on his homework.

"Aren't you done with that outfit yet?" his mother asked when he came down to dinner in it.

"Almost," Jason mumbled.

"You're going to have to wear even more of those dollar signs tomorrow," Stewart taunted. "I heard on the radio that the national debt goes up every day."

Jason gave him a four-million-dollar dirty look.

4

"**M**ay I be excused?" Jason asked when he'd finished dessert.

"Excused?" Stewart sniffed. "There's no excuse for stupidity. Next thing we know you'll pretend to be a birthday party—and go to school in your birthday suit."

Mrs. Nozzle ignored him. "Yes, you're excused, Jason. Just make sure you do your homework."

Jason had already done his homework, but he didn't want to waste time mentioning it. He had finished early because he had no idea how long it would take him to do whatever it was that Dr. Silverfish had in store for him. He just hoped it didn't have anything to do with going to school in his birthday suit—or in his dollar-feathers.

Welcome back! That's quite an impressive outfit you have on. It makes you look wealthier somehow. Richer. Almost like a multimillionaire.

Your friends must be incredibly jealous. It is a well-known fact that nothing gets people angrier than seeing other people show off their money.

But now you know you can handle it! So what if spiteful backbiters point to you and say, "There goes that jerk who's always showing off that expensive car and those expensive clothes and that expensive jewelry and those expensive hamburgers with ketchup and expensive onions on top and expensive pumpkins on the side!" You won't mind a bit, because you've learned how to put up with the snide remarks of plain old ordinary everyday non-millionaires!

Why, if I were you, I think I'd wear that wonderful dollar-sign outfit ev-

ery day of my life just to show what I thought of those jealous unrich folks, nyah, nyah-nyah, nyah, nyah.

Jason shuddered. He read on.

But I'm not you, and maybe you'd prefer to wear something else. I personally recommend something in gold, silver, platinum, or pumpkin. But that's your decision. If you wish to change your clothes, please do so now.

With a loud whoop, Jason whipped off his shirt and pants. He didn't want to waste time undoing all the safety pins, so he changed into an unfeathered T-shirt and jeans. Maybe Dr. Silverfish liked wearing dollar signs, but Jason was glad to be rid of them.

He smiled at himself in the mirror. He had passed the first day of the course with flying colors. He felt terrific. He picked up the book.

CHAPTER FIVE

You've Got What It Takes!

Perhaps you have heard the saying, "It takes money to make money." Well, now it's time to find out for yourself. Tomorrow morning, go to your bank the moment it opens. Please withdraw three million dollars. Not a penny less!

Jason didn't feel terrific anymore. He felt terrible. He didn't have three million dollars in his bank account. He didn't have two million dollars in his bank account. He didn't even have one million dollars in his bank account. He had exactly fifty-two dollars and fifty-seven cents, and he wasn't allowed to touch that except for emergencies. How could Professor Silverfish ask him to do something totally impossible? He read on.

Aha! You think that's totally impossible! You're going to tell me you don't have three million dollars in your bank account!

Well, I'm not going to let a few million missing dollars stand in your way. So how about two dollars? Surely you can put your hands on two measly smackers right this minute?

Jason emptied his pockets. Now that he'd lost his allowance, two dollar bills—a crisp new one and a sad-looking wrinkled one—were all the money he had. They were his lunch money for tomorrow. But he'd go without lunch if he had to.

Wonderful! With two dollars and some hard work you can get somewhere. Please turn the page.

Jason did.

First, find a secret spot outdoors and dig a hole in the ground there. You must dig for one full hour—not a minute less. That's the hard work part.
Next, put a single dollar bill in the bottom of the hole. *Do not use coins for this!!!* Fill the hole back up again.
Finally, take a dollar's worth of coins—

do not use bills!!!—**and sprinkle them on top of the hole. Work them into the soil to help fertilize it.**

Perhaps you have heard that money doesn't grow on trees. Well, maybe it does, and maybe it doesn't. Maybe it grows on bushes like blueberries. Maybe it grows on vines like pumpkins. Maybe it grows underground like potatoes! How can you be sure unless you give it a try?

I want you to create your very own personal money plantation. So get moving! Dig in! When you're done, come back and read the next page.

Jason closed the book and ran to his brother's door. "Do you have change for a dollar?" Jason shouted through it.

Stewart opened the door. "Regular clothes!" he said sarcastically. "What happened to Mr. National Debt?"

Jason frowned. "Never mind. Can I have that change?"

"Kind of a letdown: You were a trillion dollars, and now you're just a kid who needs change for a one."

Jason scowled at him. "Please?"

Stewart searched his pockets. "Let's see: a quarter, two nickels, and a dime. That's all I've got, unless you want the rest in pennies."

Pennies would be a real nuisance, Jason thought, but maybe they'd fertilize the soil more evenly. "I'll take 'em," he said, handing over the sad-looking dollar bill.

Stewart gave Jason the coins from his pocket. He fished fifty-five pennies out of a deep bowl on his desk. But Jason wasn't about to lose out on four million dollars because of a missing cent or two. He carefully began counting the pennies himself.

"Come on," Stewart complained. "They're all there."

"Thirteen . . . fourteen . . . fifteen—I'm just making sure," Jason replied.

"They're all there," Stewart repeated. "I'm positive."

"Now you made me lose count," Jason said. "Where was I?"

"On some other planet." Stewart sighed. Jason started over from one.

Stewart was right. All the pennies were there.

When Jason finished counting them, he gathered them up and put them in his pocket. "Thanks," he said. "I really needed these."

"You're welcome," Stewart told him. "Just don't wear them down to breakfast."

As he went to the garage for the shovel, Jason thought about secret spots. There wasn't anything secret about his yard, and his mom wouldn't want him to dig there anyway. So Jason carried the shovel up to the park and down a trail into the woods.

He searched awhile before he found the perfect spot. It was deep in the woods. You couldn't see it from the street, because tall maples and oaks surrounded it. It was the perfect place for a money tree—or a money bush, a money vine, or a money potato plant.

Jason looked at his watch. It said 6:47. He picked up the shovel and plunged it into the earth.

Dr. Silverfish had been right about the hard work part. The ground was mostly rocks. Even when Jason jumped on the shovel with both feet, it barely sank into the earth.

But Jason kept at it. After half an hour he

had managed to dig a very small hole. Sweat was pouring down his forehead. Little blisters hurt his index fingers.

Half an hour after that, he had dug a bigger hole. Sweat was pouring out of his entire body. Big blisters ached on four of his fingers and both of his thumbs. Jason thought that if it took this much work to make four million dollars, maybe he'd settle for two million.

At exactly 7:48 he put down the shovel and stopped digging in the ground. Instead he dug his hand into his pocket—oh, did that hurt his blisters!—and took out his crisp dollar bill. He stood over the hole and let the bill flutter to the bottom.

Jason stared at it for a long moment. He wiped his brow and began shoveling dirt back in. When he was all through, he took out his coins and sprinkled them on the ground. He used the shovel to work them into the soil. When they had disappeared, he patted down the dirt to make things neater.

Jason stood back and took a look. The spot seemed pretty secret, but not so secret that he couldn't find it again. He just hoped some ani-

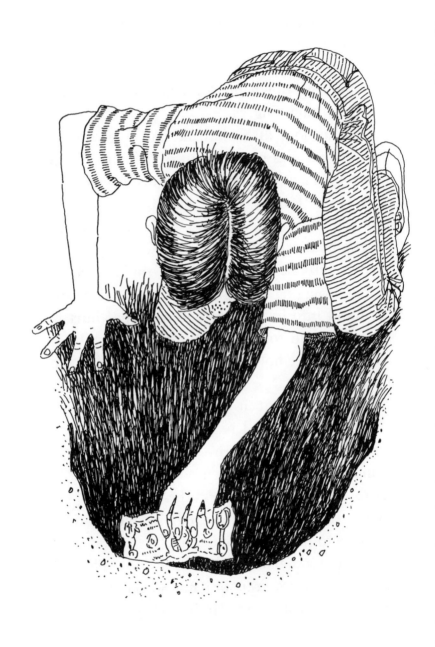

mal like a gopher or a rat or his neighbor's dog or his brother Stewart wouldn't dig up his dollar bill and coins somehow and run off with them.

Tired and filthy, Jason took the shovel back home and put it away. He couldn't remember being more exhausted in his entire life. All he wanted was a nice long shower. But first he remembered to read the next page of Dr. Silverfish's book.

> **Whew! See what I mean by hard work? I'm worn out just from looking at you! But hard work is essential if a four-millionaire is what you want to be.**
>
> **Now that you've created your money plantation, make sure you don't look at it again until I tell you to. Thank you very much.**

"You're welcome," Jason said almost in spite of himself.

> **Now it's time to learn how to save money. You can't expect to have four**

**million dollars if cash keeps slipping
through your fingers!**

**So from now until tomorrow morning,
you must save every possible penny.
I do not want you to waste a single
solitary cent.**

Jason sighed. At least that sounded easy. It
was too late to go anywhere, and he was too
exhausted besides. There was no way he could
possibly spend a cent before morning.

**Of course, not spending isn't all
there is to saving. You mustn't do
anything that might cost money. You
must not eat or drink. You must not
wash your hands and waste soap and
water and towel fibers. You must not
brush your teeth and waste toothpaste and toothbrush bristles. You must
not blow your nose and waste tissues.
You must not walk around and wear
out your shoes and clothing. You must
not use the lights or the radio or anything else that takes expensive
electricity.**

So here's what I want you to do:

Take your clothes off, get into bed, and lie in the dark. Be sure to move as little as possible, to avoid wearing out the sheets. That way, you'll save every possible penny!

See you in the A.M.!

P.S. It is okay to use the toilet. Even four-millionaires do that once in a while!

Jason groaned. Making four million dollars was getting to be harder than he'd guessed. He felt grimy and sticky and sweaty. He didn't smell so hot. And now he couldn't waste even a drop of water to clean himself up. It wasn't fair. It wasn't right. But it was Dr. Silverfish's orders.

Still, Jason had come too far to quit now. He heard his Monster Rooster alarm clock ticking away. He opened it up and took out the batteries so they wouldn't be wasted. Then he took off all his clothes, turned off the lights, slithered into bed, and tried not to move a muscle.

A moment later he heard a knock on his door. Jason hesitated. He decided that answering the door wouldn't cost anything but breath, and at least that was free. "Who is it?"

"Mom."

"What do you want?" Jason asked suspiciously.

"I want to know why you're acting so strangely."

"I'm not acting strangely."

"I just want to come in and talk to you, okay?"

"I guess."

Mrs. Nozzle came through the door and switched on the light. "Turn off the light, Mom! Quick!" Jason shouted.

"Jason, I'm not going to stand around talking in the dark."

Well, I warned her, Jason thought. *She's* the one who's wasting the electricity, not me.

"Are you all right?" asked his mom.

"Yeah," Jason said. "Fine."

"You don't usually go to bed without your bedtime snack. Or saying goodnight. You sure you're feeling okay?"

"Sure," Jason said. "I'm just a little tired, is all."

Mrs. Nozzle glanced at a book on Jason's desk. She picked it up. *"Make Four Million Dollars by Next Thursday!"* she exclaimed. "Are you reading this?"

Jason wished he could get up and grab the book from her hands. But all he could do was slink down beneath the covers and say, "Uh, sort of . . ."

Mrs. Nozzle flipped through the book, stopping now and then. "Hmmmm," she said. "Looks like you've been following the instructions pretty well. Is that why these jeans are so filthy?"

Jason squirmed a little. Then he realized squirming might wear out the sheets. He stopped squirming and nodded.

"What do you want with four million dollars, anyway?" his mother asked.

Jason started to shrug, then decided he'd better not. "Why do you play the million-dollar lottery every week?" he asked.

Mrs. Nozzle wrinkled her nose and sighed. "Good question. You got me, pardner."

"Well?" Jason pressed.

"I guess the idea of getting rich quick is pretty hard to resist," said his mother. "But getting rich quick isn't easy."

"That's for sure!" Jason agreed.

"In fact, for most people, it's impossible," she added.

"You just wait," Jason told her. "After Thursday, I'll give you some of my money. Maybe you'll be able to stop working so hard."

Mrs. Nozzle put the book down. "Well, I sure hope you're right about that. Anyhow, good luck." She kissed Jason on the forehead and walked toward the door. "I'm turning out the lights so you won't have to get up and wear out the carpet."

"Thanks," Jason replied. "Oh, Mom?"

"Yes?"

"Don't tell Stewart about this, okay?"

Mrs. Nozzle nodded and pretended to zip her lip.

"Thanks," Jason said. Then the lights went out.

Saving money is actually pretty easy, Jason thought at first. But then his stomach began to miss his bedtime snack. And when he heard Stewart out in the hallway and remembered the joke about going to school in his birthday suit, Jason shuddered.

The way things were going there was just no telling: What if Dr. Silverfish made him keep up this savings routine? What if he had to walk around in his birthday suit all day tomorrow?

5

"**J**ason! Aren't you up yet?"

Mrs. Nozzle's shouts woke Jason from dollar-filled dreams. It was Tuesday morning. With his alarm clock out of commission, Jason had overslept.

"I'm up!" he shouted back.

Remembering not to turn on any lights, Jason reached for Dr. Silverfish's book. He was glad the sunlight coming into his room was bright enough to read by.

CHAPTER SIX

You're Closer Than Ever!

Wait a minute! You dare consult the great Dr. K. Pinkerton Silverfish

without any clothes on? I'm shocked! Shocked!

Jason grabbed his bathrobe and went back to the book.

Thank you.

And congratulations! You've saved as much money in one night as any human being possibly can! This will come in very handy once you're a four-millionaire.

But simply saving money won't make you rich overnight. Or even overday. So you have my permission to eat, drink, wear clothes, turn on the lights, and even take a shower—which is something I personally recommend. You don't smell so hot.

But while you are doing those things and anything else you have in mind, you must concentrate fully and totally on your goal of four million dollars. Do not allow anything or anyone to distract you and disrupt your concentration. Avoid unnecessary conversation. Ignore unimportant matters. Think

money and only money! Consult me this afternoon.

Jason sighed. At least he didn't have to go to school in dollar signs or his birthday suit. All he had to do was concentrate fully and totally on four million dollars.

Jason was absolutely determined not to let anything distract him. When he stepped into the shower, he was concentrating so hard on money that he barely noticed how good the water felt or how much better he smelled or how hard his brother was banging on the bathroom door.

"Well!" said Stewart when Jason sat down to breakfast. "Back to almost normal! I thought today you might be wearing piggy banks all over you."

Jason didn't answer. He kept four million dollars floating right in front of him. Everything else just faded into the background.

"What's wrong?" Stewart demanded. "Did your tongue fall out?"

Jason just grunted.

"Don't tease Jason," said Mrs. Nozzle. "He's

got a lot on his mind. I'm sure he'll be all right soon."

"All right? Jason?" Stewart snorted. "That'd be a first!"

Jason ignored them. *Concentrate!* he told himself. Four million dollars. Four million dollars. Four million dollars.

But Jason's concentration did not go over well at school. It was bad enough that kids were calling him Dollar Bill or Money-Chasin' Jason to make fun of his outfit from the day before. It was worse that when his friends, like Ravi, tried to be helpful, Jason had to grunt and pretend not to notice them. But worst of all was having his lunch money buried in his secret spot.

Jason concentrated through his terrible hunger. He concentrated so hard it gave him a headache. He concentrated so hard he kept bumping into people because he didn't even notice them.

In gym class, he missed three balls in left field, tried to bat out of order, and nearly got beaned, all because he had put everything out of his mind except four million dollars. And when teachers called on him, Jason just grunted and pretended he didn't know the answers, even though he knew he would have known them if he could have thought about anything but four million dollars.

Four million dollars! Four million dollars! It was like a dumb TV jingle he couldn't get out of his mind. When he got home and picked up Dr. Silverfish's book, the only words he could see on the cover were *Four Million Dollar$!* He barely managed to open it to the right page.

CHAPTER SEVEN

Adopt a Rich Attitude!

You there! Wake up! Hey! You! PLEASE STOP CONCENTRATING ON FOUR MILLION DOLLARS RIGHT THIS INSTANT!

Jason felt as though he had emerged from a trance. He shook the cobwebs from his brain and turned back to the book.

Thank you for concentrating so hard. After all, to become a four-millionaire,

**concentrating on your goal is highly
important. You've proven you can do
it. You're closer to your goal than ever.**

**But you will need to regain your
energy for the next step, so please
concentrate now on a snack.**

Jason had no trouble taking that advice. He
went to the kitchen and grabbed himself a hand-
ful of oatmeal-carrot cookies and a glass of
papaya-parsley juice. Then he went back to his
room and picked up the book.

**The next step is simple. The next
step is easy. The next step will solve
all your money problems instantly.
Please turn the page to find out all about
it.**

Jason did.

**First, find a warm, sharing person
with eight million dollars or more.
Then simply propose marriage!**

Dr. Silverfish had to be kidding. Jason didn't know anybody who had eight million dollars. Besides, he wasn't old enough to get married. He looked back at the book.

Be sure you hold the wedding by the day after tomorrow. And congratulations! You make a wonderful couple!*

Dr. Silverfish *wasn't* kidding! Jason was so flabbergasted that he nearly missed the asterisk at the end of the sentence. He looked down to the bottom of the page.

*Alternate Method

The editors of this book have informed me that some of my readers may already be married or be too young to marry legally. Personally, I think that's ridiculous: Let those readers grow up or get divorced!

But maybe you can't grow up or get divorced by Thursday. So I hereby offer you an alternate method that will work every bit as well as the other one. Here it comes . . .

**Go to the mansion of the richest
people you can think of and ask them
to adopt you.**

Jason shook his head in disbelief. He liked his
family—well, except for his brother some of the
time. How could he desert them and go live
with rich people he didn't even know? He looked
back at the book.

**Do you want to be a four-millionaire
or don't you? By this time tomorrow
you must take one of these steps—
marriage or adoption, I don't care
which.**
**Oh, yes: Take this book along with
you. You'll need it in your new home,
future four-millionaire!**

Jason closed the book quietly. Who were the
richest people he could think of? He could think
of pretty rich baseball players. Some of them
made millions of dollars a year. But the owners
of the teams were probably even richer, since
they paid the players.

Then he remembered somebody still richer: a real estate tycoon he'd seen on that TV show, *Rich People and Their Expensive Stuff.* The tycoon owned seventeen buildings, half a dozen mansions, five yachts, lots and lots of amazing cars, and so many other expensive things Jason couldn't remember them all.

There was just one problem: All of that tycoon's mansions were thousands of miles from Jason's house. Jason glanced back at the book. He noticed a few words he had missed before.

Of course I mean rich people where you live. Now quit wasting time and get going!

Jason thought about the mansions in town. Most were up on the hill, but hardly any rich people lived in them anymore. One was part of the hospital. Another was a senior citizens' home. A couple had been turned into offices.

Then Jason remembered the Portentous Mansion. It was definitely the biggest house he could think of. And the Portentouses were not just rich. They were *very* rich. Everybody in town knew that.

Jason wasted no time. He put on his jacket, grabbed the book, and hurried out the door.

His brother was coming up the walk. "Where are you headed?" he asked cheerfully.

Jason felt slightly uncomfortable. "Uh, just for a walk."

"What's that book with all the dollar signs on it?" Stewart grabbed it right out of Jason's hands. *"Make Four Million Dollars by Next Thursday?* What are you supposed to do—rob a bank?"

Jason grabbed it back. "Never mind," he said uncomfortably. "Just, uh, tell Mom I, uh, may be late for dinner."

"Sure you'll be late. They'll probably arrest you and throw you in jail."

Jason scowled. "Very funny."

"How late?" Stewart asked.

Jason hesitated. If the Portentous family adopted him, he might *never* come home for dinner. The thought made him feel slightly sick to his stomach. "Just late," he said with a catch in his throat, and ran down the street.

The mansion district wasn't far. Once Jason

left his own neighborhood, the houses kept getting bigger and bigger. Soon he was walking past nothing but mansions. And then came the hugest one of all.

At the far end of a lawn the size of a football field loomed the Portentous Mansion. The stone house was even bigger than Jason had remembered. At one side a long driveway led up to an eighteen-car garage. A huge swimming pool peeked out from the backyard. A fence of iron bars surrounded the property.

To the left of the front gate was a silver plate with a name engraved in it:

PORTENTOUS

Just below the plate was what looked like a doorbell button. Jason hesitated, then pressed it hard.

No answer. Jason pressed the button again.

Still no answer. Jason pressed the button one more time. An instant later he heard whirring above his head. He looked up. The eye of a camera was aiming right at him. He guessed the Portentouses had some kind of TV security system.

"What do you want?" asked a curt voice that came from a little loudspeaker just above Jason's head.

Jason took a deep breath. "I—uh—want to talk to somebody."

"Speak into the loudspeaker, please," said the voice.

"I said I want to talk to somebody."

"About what, please?"

Jason could barely get the words out. "About —about getting adopted."

He heard giggles from the loudspeaker. He heard the words, "Please wait." Then he heard a loud *click*.

For a long time nothing seemed to happen. As Jason aimed his finger at the button again, he saw a girl and a boy come out the front door at the other end of the lawn. They stepped into a little electric cart. They drove directly toward Jason.

Jason shuddered. He wished he were somewhere else—anywhere! But he also wished he had washed up and brushed his teeth and put on his best clothes before coming here. He tried to smooth his hair so he'd look more like a kid somebody might want to adopt.

The cart pulled up to the other side of the gate. The boy and the girl stared out at him through the black iron bars. The boy looked about Jason's age, and the girl about as old as Stewart. But they acted much older—almost like parents. Part of it was their matching dark-blue private-school uniforms, Jason thought. But part of it had nothing to do with what they were wearing. The sour looks on their faces hinted that they might have been eating too many fish eggs.

"Who are you?" the boy sniffed.

Jason tried to smile. "Jason Nozzle."

"What are you doing here?" the girl demanded.

Jason's throat felt as though a spider were crawling down it. "I—I—I . . . want your family to . . . adopt me," he stammered.

"Adopt you?" The boy laughed. "Whyever should we do that?"

Jason hemmed and hawed.

"It's because you want to be rich, isn't it?" the girl prodded.

Jason couldn't open his mouth to answer.

"You're a panic!" The boy snorted. "Give us

one good reason why we should take you into our family."

Jason couldn't think of one.

"You're a very silly boy," said the girl, in the very same tone Jason's grandmother used when he was very little. "You just want to be rich, that's all. You're not the first who's tried it."

The boy grinned and pointed to Jason's book. "We've certainly seen *that* before."

"Dozens of times," agreed the girl.

"And if we adopted every child who came here and wanted us to share our money, we wouldn't have any left for ourselves, would we?" the boy demanded.

"Our family made its money the old-fashioned way," the girl declared. "The same way our grandparents did. We inherited it."

"That means our parents got it from their parents," the boy pointed out.

"I know what that means," Jason said. "I may not be rich, but I'm not stupid."

"Well, you certainly fooled us!" The girl laughed.

"Go!" said the boy. "We've got nothing for

you here. Shoo! Skedaddle!" He shook his fist at Jason.

As Jason backed away, he tripped on the curb and fell into the street. The boy and the girl hooted at him. "Another poor fool!" the girl cackled.

"They *all* want our money!" the boy agreed.

"How pitiful!" said the girl. "How sad!" She drove the cart back toward the house.

Jason took a last glance back through the bars of the mansion's iron fence. Then he picked himself up and trudged home. He had failed in his mission so far. But he still had until late tomorrow to try to get some rich person to adopt him.

But even though he had failed, Jason suddenly felt relieved. He couldn't imagine living with the Portentouses, no matter how rich they were. His own family wasn't rich, but at least it wasn't a bunch of stuck-up sourballs.

When he came through the front door, his mother and brother were sitting down to dinner. "We didn't put out food for you," Mrs. Nozzle said.

"You did say you thought you'd be late," Stewart reminded him.

"Guess I thought wrong," Jason replied with a shrug. He took his plate to the kitchen and spooned out big helpings of parsnip quiche and spaghetti with spinach sauce. He was happy to be home—even if his brother kept making snide remarks about "Mr. Millions" and "Mr. Moneybags" all through dinner.

Still, Jason kept running plans through his head. Maybe after dinner he could get some rich people to adopt him. Better yet, maybe he could even get them to adopt his whole family. That would keep the four million dollars from slipping through his fingers.

But when he went to his room, he suddenly realized he had let something else slip through his fingers. Dr. Silverfish's book was missing!

Missing? Jason couldn't believe it. It couldn't be. By the time he finished searching his room, it looked as though a tornado had struck, followed by a buffalo stampede. But the book was nowhere to be found.

Maybe his brother had taken it. No, not a chance, Jason realized. Stewart was at the dinner table when he came home. He was still there now.

Jason thought back. He knew he had the book when he talked to the Portentous kids. But he didn't remember bringing it home.

Of course! He must have dropped the book when he tripped and fell outside the mansion!

Jason cursed himself for being so careless. First his entire allowance and now the book that would make him rich! Maybe he was on his way to losing his mind.

Jason grabbed his jacket, dashed outside, and retraced his steps. He kept an eye out for the book in case he might have dropped it on the way home. But he still hadn't found it when he saw the Portentous mansion in the distance.

Jason ran up to the gates. He looked all around. But there was no sign of *Make Four Million Dollars by Next Thursday!*

Maybe the Portentous kids had seen it and picked it up. Jason rang the bell. The camera whirred above his head. But nobody answered. Maybe nobody was home. Or maybe somebody was avoiding Jason.

Jason rang again and again, but nobody responded—not even the camera. The book was gone—along with his chance for four million dollars.

Jason kept looking for the book as he trudged home. Maybe, maybe, maybe . . . but none of the maybes came true.

Jason felt horrible as he put the batteries back in his Monster Rooster alarm clock. When he fell asleep, four million dollars began dancing in his brain. They mocked him. They told him he wasn't good enough for them. They told him to give up.

Jason woke with a start. He'd find the book somehow. He'd get another copy somewhere. He wasn't about to give up.

He glanced at the clock. It was almost midnight. Thursday was the day after tomorrow. One way or another, Jason was still determined to be a four-millionaire by then.

6

Wednesday morning, Jason woke up from a night of lousy dreams. He was prepared for the worst.

"No crazy outfit today? And you're actually speaking to us?" his brother joked at breakfast.

"Lay off, okay?" Jason said angrily.

"Fine," Stewart replied. "I just hope you'll be a little more cheerful if you make all those millions you're trying for."

Jason didn't answer. He didn't feel like arguing. He didn't eat much breakfast. He didn't stop by Ravi's house on the way to school. He wanted to be at school the second it opened.

The moment the doors were unlocked, Jason ran to the library. He checked the card catalog.

It didn't list any book called *Make Four Million Dollars by Next Thursday!* It didn't list any books by anyone named Silverfish.

Jason sighed. He'd just have to wait until after school. Then he'd phone the library downtown and the bookstore at the mall and see if they had copies of the book.

Jason didn't want to think about what would happen if they didn't. To put it out of his mind, he concentrated on his schoolwork. A couple of the teachers actually said "Welcome back!" as though he'd been in outer space or something.

Jason let the kids and the teachers have their jokes. There was still a chance that by tomorrow he'd have four million dollars—and the last laugh.

But the rest of the day, Jason didn't feel much like laughing. Every time he remembered how stupid he was to have lost the book, he got an awful feeling in the pit of his stomach.

"Are you sure you're all right?" Ravi asked him after school. "You didn't eat anything at lunch."

"I'm fine," Jason told him in a crabby tone of voice. "Sort of."

"Fine?" Ravi said. "You've been totally weird since the beginning of the week!"

"Don't worry about me," Jason told him. "I'm going to be—who's that?"

Jason turned around. A boy from an older class was shouting "Wait up!" and running toward him.

Jason recognized the boy from baseball. His name was Milo Crinkley. The reason Jason remembered him was that Milo had once made nine errors in a single game. For a while in Jason's league, an error was known as a "crinkle."

Milo caught up with Jason and Ravi. "Are you the kid who wore all those dollar signs the other day?" Milo asked.

Jason prepared himself for some kind of bad joke. "Maybe," he said suspiciously.

"Are you the one who kept bumping into people in the hallways?"

"So what if he was?" Ravi challenged.

Milo put his hand on Jason's shoulder. "I need to talk to you alone."

"I'm his best friend," Ravi said indignantly. "We don't keep secrets."

"This is private," Milo told Jason. "If you

want to tell your friend about it afterward, that's up to you."

"I'd better see what this is about," Jason told Ravi.

"Okay. But I'm keeping an eye out in case this guy tries to start something," Ravi declared.

Milo took Jason aside. He took off his bookpack. A brown paper bag fell out and crashed to the sidewalk.

Another crinkle, Milo thought, but he kept it to himself.

Milo picked up the bag and handed it to Jason. "I think this might be yours."

Jason looked at the bag suspiciously. "What's in here? Some kind of gag?"

"Open it," Milo told him.

Jason did. Inside was a copy of *Make Four Million Dollars by Next Thursday!*

Jason couldn't believe his luck. It was his own copy. He could tell from all the flecks of mud on it. "It's mine, all right!"

"Thought so. I put it in the bag in case you didn't want to show anybody else."

"Where'd you find it?"

"I was out riding my bike last night. I ran over it by accident."

Jason noticed fresh tire marks on the cover. "How'd you know it was mine?"

"Oh, I've been watching you for a couple of days. I had the feeling you might have had something to do with that Silverfish guy."

"Did you make four million dollars?" Jason asked. "Are you rich?"

"Not me!" Milo laughed. "I'm perfect."

"Huh?" Jason said.

Milo grinned. "Just kidding. I mean, I never read that book of yours. I read a different one by Dr. Silverfish. He's kind of weird, but he's pretty smart, too."

"Yeah. I'm finding that out," Jason agreed. "Anyhow, thanks. Thanks a lot."

Milo laughed. "Thank me again when you're rich. Good luck!" He slung his bookpack over his shoulders and went on his way.

"What was that all about?" Ravi asked Jason.

"Nothing. He found something of mine, that's all."

"The something in that bag?"

Jason nodded. "My secret mission. If it goes right, you'll know all about it soon enough."

Ravi shook his head. "I guess I was wrong about secrets."

"If I could tell you, I would," Jason said. "Believe me, I would! But it'll all be over tomorrow."

"You mean you'll be normal again?"

Would being a multimillionaire be normal? "Sort of," Jason decided.

When he got home, Jason took the book straight up to his room. But as he sat down on his bed, he remembered that he hadn't managed to get adopted. He wasn't sure Dr. Silverfish would understand. The doctor might scold him for having lost the book, even if he had gotten it back again. Jason opened the book timidly, worriedly, slowly.

CHAPTER EIGHT

The Rest Is Easy!

So you're happily and richly married!

Jason shook his head.

No? Then you've found a wealthy new family!

Jason shook his head again.

Neither one? Good for you!

I wouldn't have the slightest respect for anyone who'd stoop so low as to marry for money. And as for picking your relatives—well, there are plenty of things you can pick, but your family isn't one of them. You're more or less stuck with the relatives you've got, even if they're not multimillionaires. You may as well get used to 'em.

So you have shown excellent judgment. And showing excellent judgment is crucial to becoming a multimillionaire.

Jason's chest puffed out a little. He had succeeded in spite of himself. He couldn't possibly fail now!

You're on the home stretch. I hope I don't have to remind you that tomorrow is Thursday!

And your task for this evening is simple. You must spend from now until midnight chanting for wealth. This will demand the most concentration you have ever mustered up.

Sit with your legs crossed on the floor of a darkened room. Say out loud, "I need four million dollars." Count "One," in your head. Say, "I need four million dollars." Count "Two," but don't say it. Keep chanting out loud and counting in your head until the stroke of midnight. Then it will be Thursday morning, and you will return to this book.

Jason turned out the lights, sat down on the floor, and crossed his legs. "I want four million dollars," he said, and thought *One*.

"I want four million dollars," he said, and thought *Two*.

"I want four million dollars," he said, and thought *Three*.

It was the most boring thing Jason had ever done. By the end of the first hour, he wanted to do anything but sit there saying "I want four million dollars," and thinking *Two thousand seven hundred and sixty-six*. But he was too close to stop now.

He kept one eye on his Monster Rooster alarm clock. There were still eight hours till midnight. He began to chant faster and faster. Maybe it would be less boring that way.

". . . I need four million dollars."

Three thousand seven hundred and twenty-four . . .

". . . Ineedfourmilliondollars."

Fourthousandtwohundredtwentysix . . .

". . . Ineefrmilliondolrs."

Fivethousaneighthunnerfiftyfi . . .

". . . Neefrmilliondlrs."

Sixthousantwohunredsixtythree . . .

". . . Neef . . ."

. . . Jason woke with a start. His legs were still crossed. He looked around. The sun was up outside. He checked his rooster clock. It was just past 6 A.M.

Jason shuddered. Sometime during the night he must have begun dreaming about chanting. He hadn't actually been chanting at all. He hadn't chanted until midnight. He had failed.

But then the last time he thought he'd failed, Dr. Silverfish had congratulated him on his excellent judgment. Maybe he hadn't failed after all.

Jason looked around. He didn't see four million dollars anywhere. Maybe he *had* failed. He picked up Dr. Silverfish's book.

<u>It's Thursday!</u>

Did you chant your way to wealth?

Jason slowly shook his head no.

Of course you didn't! No human being in his or her right mind could possibly sit in one place and chant for four million dollars for hours on end without falling asleep!

Jason smiled and nodded. Maybe this was going to come out all right after all.

This proves there is something you needed more than four million dollars! You needed to stop that silly chanting and do something interesting!

Good for you! You have just learned that there are more important things

than sacrificing everything for money. PLEASE turn the page!

Jason did.

Well, what are you waiting for? Go get your shovel and attend to your money plantation! And take this book along with you!

Jason had forgotten all about his money plantation. Now he could almost see it growing—a money tree as tall as Jack's beanstalk and twice as green, with four million dollars worth of leaves just waiting to be picked.

He got dressed in record time, making sure to put on his sturdiest sneakers in case any climbing was involved. He didn't know exactly why he needed the shovel, but if Dr. Silverfish said to take one, it was all right with him.

Jason clutched the book tightly. He had no intention of losing it ever again.

As he ran down the street toward the park, Jason half expected to see the huge tree towering above the woods. So far it didn't seem to be

visible. He remembered what Dr. Silverfish had said about money trees. Maybe this one had come out more like a bush.

But when Jason reached the spot where he had buried his dollar and fertilized it with coins, there was no money bush. There was no money shrub. There wasn't even a money vine. There was just a patch of freshly dug earth.

But Dr. Silverfish had hinted that money might grow underground like potatoes. Of course! That was what the shovel was for!

Jason dug and dug. He found pennies, a dime, and a nickel, but he didn't even bother to pick them up. There'd be more money farther down. Big money. He was sure of it.

Jason dug frantically. He hardly noticed when his blisters began hurting again. He found a few more pennies, and then a dirty but surprisingly crisp-looking dollar bill.

He stopped digging. He realized it now: The bill was the one he had planted there. His money hadn't grown at all. In fact, he was still missing most of the coins he had buried. He opened the book in disgust.

CONGRATULATIONS!
YOU'RE A FOUR-MILLIONAIRE!

I knew you could do it!

Unless by some strange chance something unusual has gone wrong. In which case, please turn the page.

Jason felt like crying. He held it back so he wouldn't drip on the book as he turned the page.

CONGRATULATIONS!
YOU'RE NOT A FOUR-MILLIONAIRE!

And what's so terrible about that? Plenty of perfectly fine people don't have four million dollars.

Do you need four million dollars to enjoy a tunafish taco or a peanut-butter-and-jelly pizza? Do you need four million dollars to collect a jarful of lightning bugs? Do you need four million dollars to dance like a gorilla or sing like a chicken or yodel like my Uncle Herman?

Of course not!

And neither do four-millionaires!

Which proves conclusively that there are more important things to worry about than the three million and umpty-ump thousand dollars you don't have.

That was easy enough for Dr. Silverfish to say, Jason thought. He already had his four million dollars!

I'll bet you're thinking, "That's easy enough for Dr. Silverfish to say. He already has four million dollars!"

Did I ever tell you any such thing? I most certainly did not! I said I'm the world's greatest expert on getting rich quick. Which I am: I know more about it than anybody else on earth. And I know that you can be happy even if you can never afford to eat pheasants' tongues with dogfish eggs or ride your own polo pony or zip around in a gold-plated, turbocharged, 990-bullpower pickup truck.

Jason frowned. He wasn't quite convinced.

Being rich doesn't have anything to do with being good. And good people are at least as much fun as rich people any day of the week!

Which would you rather do? Yodel your own yodels and catch your own lightning bugs and roast your own pumpkins, or sit around and be bored counting all the money you have and worrying about how to make more?

I thought so!

Jason felt slightly better. Just slightly. He turned the page.

DID I TELL YOU
TO TURN THE PAGE?

Jason shook his head.

Right. I did not. Well, I'll let it go this time—but only because there aren't any more pages to turn.

Thanks for being here.

Glad you could make it.

If you still want to be an instant multimillionaire, please return to page

one of this book. There you will find some excellent instructions from a brilliant fellow named Silverfish.

And now I must be going. My favorite jack-o'-lantern is making eyes at me.

Toodle-oo! Big wave! Goodbye!

P.S. Make sure you don't miss my next book, *Be Famous in a Flash!*

Jason closed the book. It was hard to tell, but the jack-o'-lantern seemed to be smiling at him from the back cover. So did Dr. Silverfish.

Jason trudged home. His mom and his brother were sitting at the breakfast table.

"Well," said Stewart, "it's Thursday. Are you a multimillionaire yet?"

"Not exactly," Jason muttered.

"Too bad," said his mother. "We certainly could have used a few million dollars around here."

"It's not all bad," Jason pointed out. "At least nobody will have to eat fish eggs around here."

That day in school, Jason was glad to be just a normal non-millionaire—a kid who wasn't wearing dollar signs all over his clothes and didn't have to concentrate on four million dollars or worry about getting rich people to adopt him. He hardly even missed the car and the yacht and the airplane and the baseball cards he'd been dreaming of.

But after school he borrowed his brother's treasure finder again. Along with the shovel and the book, he took it down to his secret spot in the woods.

Beep! Two pennies. *Brap!* A nickel. *Burp!* More pennies! Ten minutes later he had dug up all the coins he'd planted but hadn't found—all but two cents worth. Soon he gave up trying to find the last two pennies. He figured two cents was pretty cheap for a course like Dr. Silverfish's.

Jason tossed his book into the hole and covered it over with dirt. He was through with the idea of being a four-millionaire.

But not being a four-millionaire was one thing, and not having any money was another. He hated the idea of being broke. The Frozen Lizard stand reminded him of it. After all that digging, he would have loved a Lizard bar, but he was still almost out of money until the end of the month. It hadn't mattered much when he was about to become a four-millionaire. Now it mattered a lot.

Jason absentmindedly stuck his hands in his nearly-empty pockets. But they weren't as empty as he thought. He dug deeper into his jeans. Out popped two five-dollar bills and two singles.

He hadn't lost his allowance after all. He'd just left it in a different pair of pants. He shook his head. One of these days, he really would have to get organized.

But for now he walked up to the Frozen Lizard stand and ordered a Snowy Skink. As he bit into it, he noticed a couple of kids at the edge of the park. They had Snowy Skinks, too, but they didn't seem to be enjoying them. They seemed to be bored, sort of annoyed.

Jason suddenly recognized them—the Portentous kids, looking sour as ever. Maybe once you were rich, the only thing you really enjoyed eating was fish eggs.

But Jason ignored them. He didn't worry about fish eggs anymore. And he'd saved so much money in the past week that he decided to buy himself another treat. When he finished his Snowy Skink, he ordered a Frostigator. It wasn't squishy, and it didn't taste anything like ball bearings. It tasted like a million dollars—maybe even four million.

A few weeks later one of his classmates came to school in a suit of dollar signs. A genuine multimillionaire might have given her a few dollars worth of helpful advice.

But Jason decided his classmate would get four million dollars worth of helpful advice soon enough. He just crunched on a slice of peanut-butter-and-jelly pizza and softly yodeled a cowboy tune. He didn't say a word.

ABOUT THE AUTHOR

STEPHEN MANES has written more than thirty books. Children in five states have voted his best-selling *Be a Perfect Person in Just Three Days!* (to which this book is a sequel) their favorite book of the year. It is available in a Bantam Skylark paperback edition, as are his *Chicken Trek* and *It's New! It's Improved! It's Terrible!* His book *The Obnoxious Jerks* is available in Bantam Starfire hardcover and paperback editions.

Mr. Manes has written many columns and articles for *P/C Computing*, *PC Magazine*, and other computer journals. He codeveloped Bantam's *StarFixer* software and wrote *The Complete MCI Mail Handbook*. He cocreated *Encyclopedia Placematica*, the world's first book of place mats. He and his work have been featured in several public-television programs, and his screenplays have been produced for movies and television.

Mr. Manes was born in Pittsburgh, Pennsylvania. He currently lives in Seattle, Washington.

ABOUT THE ILLUSTRATOR

GEORGE ULRICH was born in Morristown, New Jersey, and received his Bachelor of Fine Arts degree from Syracuse University. He has illustrated several Bantam Skylark books, including *The Amazing Adventure of Me, Myself, and I* by Jovial Bob Stine and the books in The Never Sink Nine series by Gibbs Davis. He lives in Marblehead, Massachusetts, with his wife and two sons.